You Should!

You Should!

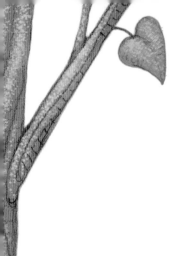

Dedicated to

the fantastic marvelous hippos, who think they "should" be flamingos. —G. T.

Published by Familius LLC, www.familius.com
Familius books are available at special discounts for bulk purchases for sales promotions, family, or corporate use. Special editions, including personalized covers, excerpts of existing books, or books with corporate logos, can be created in large quantities for special needs. For more information, contact Premium Sales at 559-876-2170 or email specialmarkets@familius.com.

Library of Congress Cataloging-in-Publication Data
2013935467
Hardcover ISBN 9781938301704   Paperback ISBN 9781945547546   eISBN 9781938301513

10 9 8 7 6 5 4 3

First Edition

Jacket and book design by David Miles.
Illustrations for this book were done with pencil on paper and scanned and painted digitally.

You Should! You Should!

WRITTEN & ILLUSTRATED
BY GINNY TILBY

FAMILIUS

You shouldn't do THAT.

Instead, you should climb this tree
and dangle upside down with me.
It's very fun, don't you agree?
This is the way that you should be.
You should! You should!

I should? Okay.
If that's what you say.
I guess I'll swim another day.

WHUMP!

What a bump!

When you walk, try this you see.

Throw your toes up, high and free.

Lift your chin and stretch your wing.

A walk like mine is just the thing.

Should I?

　　Yes, try.

Like this?

　　Reach high.

This walk is hard. I don't know why.

I should be able! . . . Shouldn't I?

You probably want a dance that's new.

Here's the perfect prance for you.

Spin and spin, round and round,

until your feet float off the ground!

Spin round, like me!

You should, you see.

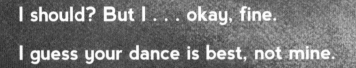

I should? But I . . . okay, fine.

I guess your dance is best, not mine.

You look hungry. Come and eat!

You should *peck-peck-peck* this treat

A hippo's CHOMP is dull and dreary.

Peck-peck-peck is bright and cheery!

Don't chomp? Okay. I should obey.

I want you to like me.

I'll *peck-peck* away.

KER-SPLAT!

I was afraid of that.

Hello there friend, you like to sing?

We'll help you sing the sweetest thing.

Open wide and shout with glee:

OO! OO! AH! AH!
EE! EE! EE!

You should! You should!

I should? Okay.

I guess I'll sing like you,

your way.

OO AA EEE!

Too much glee?

Wear this hat! You must! You must!

I'm an expert you can trust.

We'll toss your frumpy lump away.

You really must! You must, I say!

I must? Okay.

I won't delay.

Good-bye old hat that Mother made.

I guess I found a better trade.

Oh my, your spot! That spot won't do.

I've got the spot that's best for you.

My friend, you should not wear that spot!

Take it off! You really ought.

I ought?

You ought.

My spot?

Your spot.

But I cannot!

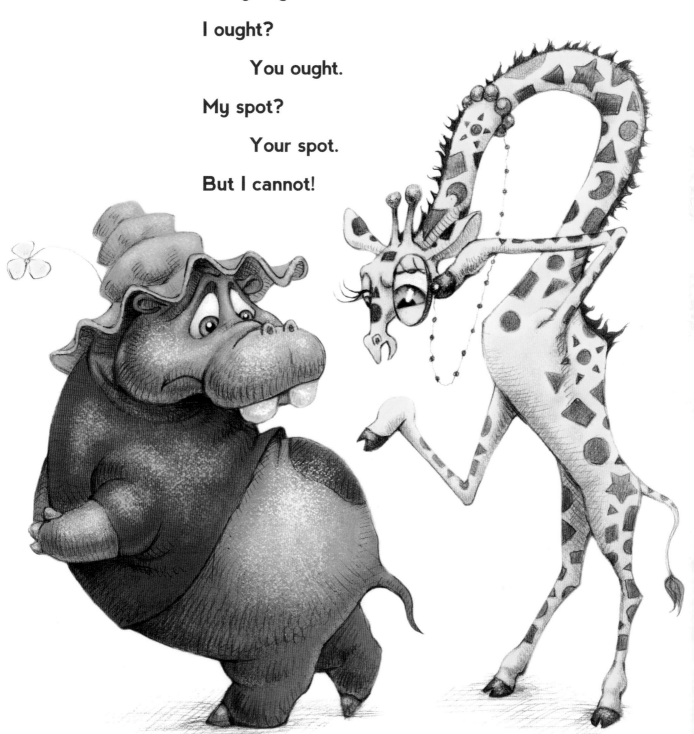

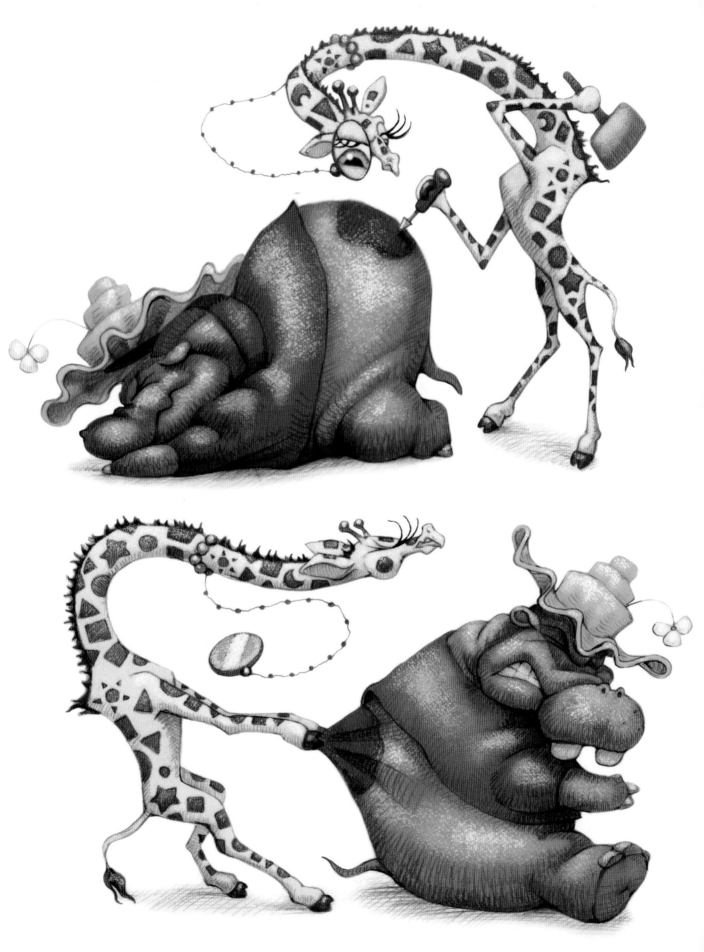

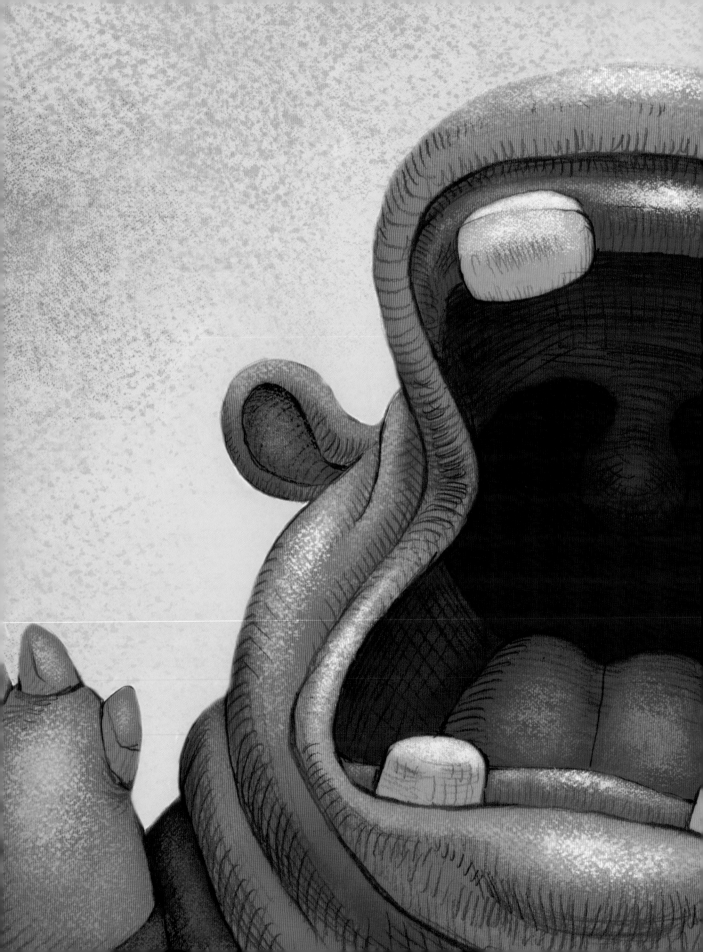

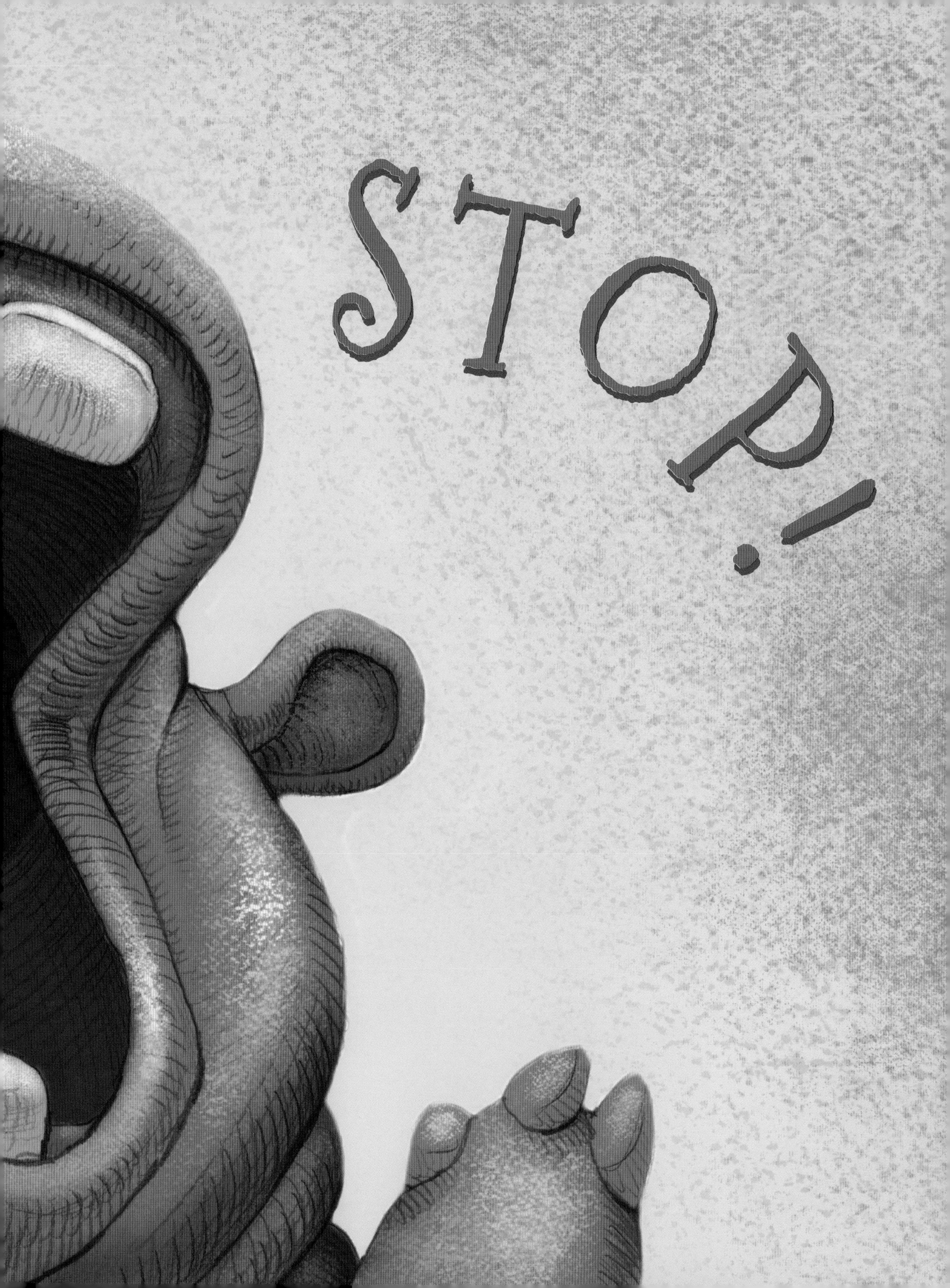
STOP!

I like my hat!

I don't want to sing like that.

I prefer my LA LA LA!

Not "oo oo, ee ee, ah ah ah."

If I *peck-peck*, I'll make a mess.

But I can CHOMP with sweet success!

Spinning does not help my feet.

I move to a different beat.

I like your walk, but that's for you.

I have a walk that's my own too.

Upside down is not for me,

and I don't like to climb, you see.

Today, I think that I would rather

swim and watch the fishes gather.

You're welcome to enjoy a ride,

and float awhile on my backside.

But I won't say, "You should! You should!"

I'll let you choose it, if you would.

'Cause very most importantly,

I am choosing to be . . .

me.